D1539514

N

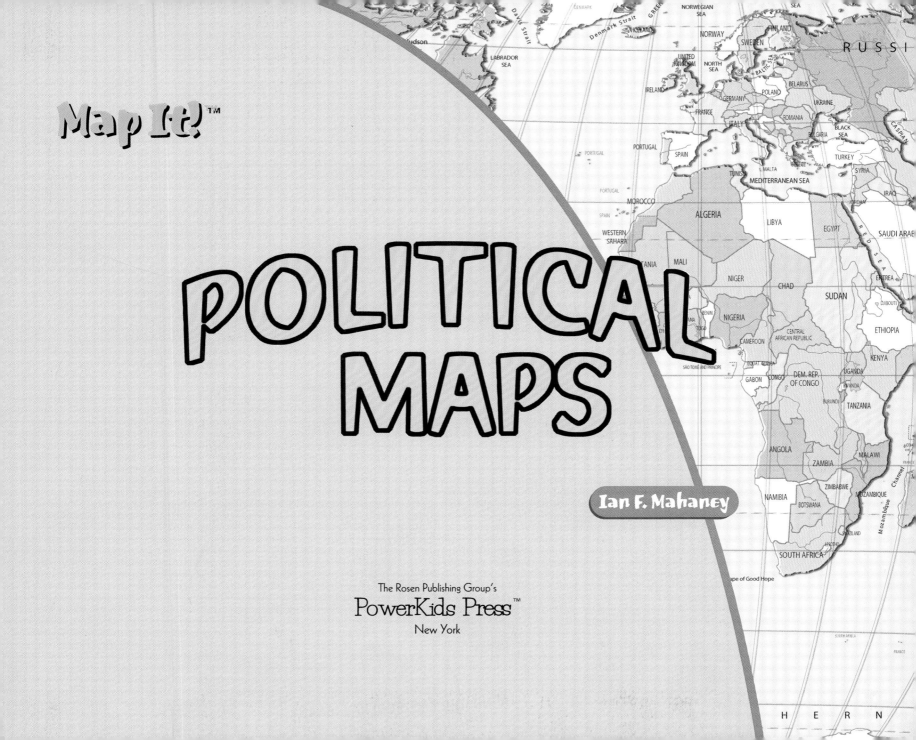

Map It!™

POLITICAL MAPS

Ian F. Mahaney

The Rosen Publishing Group's

PowerKids Press™

New York

To my parents, who still deal with me daily

Published in 2007 by The Rosen Publishing Group, Inc.
29 East 21st Street, New York, NY 10010

First Edition

Editor: Jennifer Way
Book Design: Greg Tucker
Photo Researcher: Jeffrey Wendt

Photo Credits: Cover, p. 6 Library of Congress Geography and Map Division; pp. 5, 10, 13, 21 (top) National Atlas of the United States,
http://nationalatlas.gov; pp. 14, 21 (bottom) © 2002 GeoAtlas; p. 17 Federal Election Commission; p. 18 United States Department
of Agriculture.

Library of Congress Cataloging-in-Publication Data

Mahaney, Ian F.
  Political maps / Ian F. Mahaney.— 1st ed.
     p. cm. — (Map it!)
  Includes index.
  ISBN 1-4042-3055-6 — ISBN 1-4042-2211-1 — ISBN 1-4042-2401-7
  1. Map reading—Juvenile literature. 2. Administrative and political divisions—Maps—Juvenile literature. I. Title. II. Series.

  GA130.M36 2007
  912'.014—dc22

                                            2005026343

Manufactured in the United States of America

Contents

You have seen maps. Maybe you have seen one used to explain a **political** event or the weather report on television. Have you ever wanted to learn more about maps?

Maps can help us learn a lot about the world in which we live. Different types of maps can teach us about different areas or show us the **physical** features on Earth.

Most maps have several things in common. First, maps have a **legend**. A legend is a key that helps you understand what is on the map. The legend explains what the **symbols** on the map mean. Maps also have a **scale**. A scale explains the connection between a distance on the map and the same distance on Earth. Finally, maps have a **compass rose**. A compass rose shows the four main directions on Earth. These are north, south, east, and west. In this book you will learn about political maps.

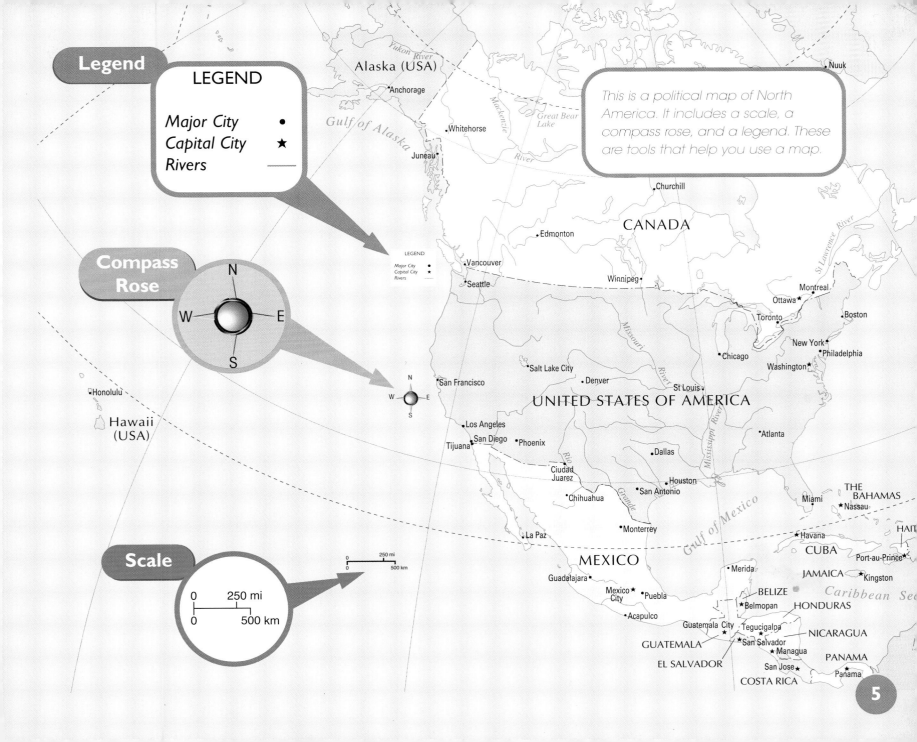

CANADA

On this political map of the United States, you can see major cities, state capitals, and the political borders between states and countries. These are all humanmade features. You can also see natural features, such as lakes and oceans.

Edmonton

Winnipeg

Quebec City

ME

Montreal

Augusta

Ottawa ★

Montpelier

NH

Helena ⊙

Idaho

Boise

Minnesota

St. Paul ⊙

Concord

VT

Toronto

Albany ⊙

MA

New York

Boston

Provi

South Dakota

Wisconsin

Michigan

RI

Wyoming

Pierre ⊙

Madison ⊙

Lansing ⊙

Hartford ⊙

CT

Salt Lake City ⊙

Cheyenne ⊙

Detroit •

Pennsylvania

New York • New York

Chicago •

Trenton

Iowa

Philadelphia

New Jersey

Utah

Nebraska

Lincoln ⊙

Des Moines ⊙

Ohio

Indiana

Columbus ⊙

Harrisburg

Dover •

MD

DE

Denver ⊙

Colorado

Illinois

Springfield ⊙

Indianapolis ⊙

West Virginia

★ Annapolis

Washington, D.C.

Topeka ⊙

Kansas

St. Louis •

Jefferson City ⊙

Frankfort ⊙

Charleston •

Richmond •

Virginia

Santa Fe ⊙

Missouri

Kentucky

Raleigh ⊙

Nashville ⊙

North Carolina

Arizona

Phoenix •

Oklahoma

Oklahoma City ⊙

Arkansas

Little Rock ⊙

Tennessee

Memphis •

Columbia ⊙

South Carolina

Atlanta ⊙

New Mexico

Dallas •

Mississippi

Alabama

Montgomery ⊙

Georgia

Texas

Louisiana

Jackson ⊙

North Atlantic Ocean

Hermosillo •

Austin ⊙

Baton Rouge ⊙

Tallahassee ⊙

Houston •

New Orleans •

Chihuahua •

Florida

MEXICO

Gulf of Mexico

Miami •

THE BAHAMAS

What Is a Political Map?

If you drove across the United States, you would see both natural and humanmade things. Bridges and roads are humanmade objects. Rivers, oceans, and mountains are examples of natural features.

Political maps show the humanmade features of Earth. Political maps mark major cities and capitals, and they show political borders. Political borders are imaginary lines that separate countries and states. If you looked at a political map of the United States, you would see the lines between states.

Political maps point out humanmade objects to help us understand how people have changed the land we are studying. To help us further understand the land that lies within political borders, political maps usually include major natural features. These can be oceans, lakes, rivers, deserts, and mountain ranges.

In order to be able to read a political map, you need to become familiar with the legend. The legend helps you understand the meaning of the lines and symbols printed on the map.

There are many symbols in the map's legend. As do all other maps, political maps use three types of symbols.

First, there are point symbols, which mark fixed points, like cities. Cities are symbolized by a black point or a small circle. Capital cities, like Washington, D.C., are noted with a special point symbol. Area symbols on a map can represent, or stand for, bigger features such as lakes, oceans, or bays. They are colored blue. Finally, there are line symbols. Line symbols show things such as rivers or borders.

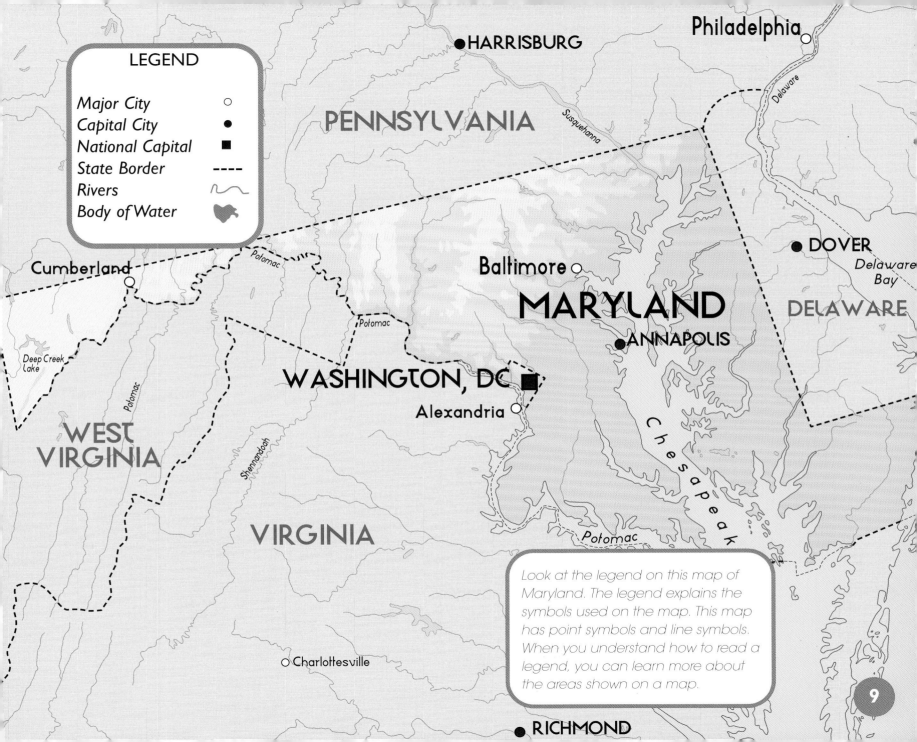

LEGEND

Major City	○
Capital City	●
National Capital	■
State Border	- - - -
Rivers	∿
Body of Water	▨

●HARRISBURG

Philadelphia○

PENNSYLVANIA

Susquehanna

Delaware

Cumberland

Potomac

Baltimore○

●DOVER

Delaware Bay

MARYLAND

DELAWARE

Potomac

Deep Creek Lake

Potomac

●ANNAPOLIS

WEST VIRGINIA

WASHINGTON, DC ■

Alexandria○

Chesapeake

Shenandoah

VIRGINIA

Potomac

Look at the legend on this map of Maryland. The legend explains the symbols used on the map. This map has point symbols and line symbols. When you understand how to read a legend, you can learn more about the areas shown on a map.

○Charlottesville

9

●RICHMOND

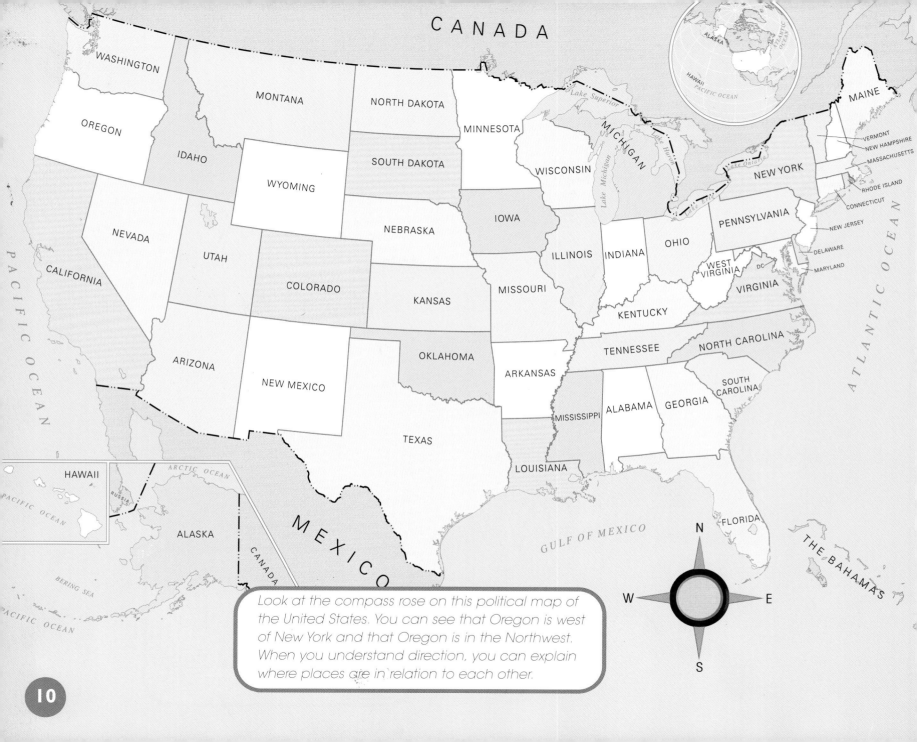

CANADA

WASHINGTON

OREGON

MONTANA

IDAHO

WYOMING

NORTH DAKOTA

SOUTH DAKOTA

MINNESOTA

Lake Superior

MICHIGAN

MAINE

NEVADA

CALIFORNIA

UTAH

COLORADO

NEBRASKA

IOWA

WISCONSIN

Lake Michigan

Lake Huron

MICHIGAN

NEW YORK

VERMONT
NEW HAMPSHIRE
MASSACHUSETTS

Lake Erie

Lake Ontario

PENNSYLVANIA

RHODE ISLAND
CONNECTICUT

NEW JERSEY

ARIZONA

NEW MEXICO

KANSAS

MISSOURI

ILLINOIS

INDIANA

OHIO

WEST
VIRGINIA

DC

DELAWARE

MARYLAND

VIRGINIA

OKLAHOMA

ARKANSAS

KENTUCKY

TENNESSEE

NORTH CAROLINA

PACIFIC OCEAN

TEXAS

MISSISSIPPI

ALABAMA

GEORGIA

SOUTH
CAROLINA

ATLANTIC OCEAN

LOUISIANA

ARCTIC OCEAN

HAWAII

RUSSIA

PACIFIC OCEAN

ALASKA

CANADA

MEXICO

GULF OF MEXICO

FLORIDA

THE BAHAMAS

BERING SEA

PACIFIC OCEAN

ALASKA
HAWAII
PACIFIC OCEAN
ATLANTIC OCEAN

N

W   E

S

Look at the compass rose on this political map of
the United States. You can see that Oregon is west
of New York and that Oregon is in the Northwest.
When you understand direction, you can explain
where places are in relation to each other.

Understanding Directions

The compass rose shows the directions north, south, east, and west on the map. Find the compass rose on this political map. The arrow pointing up is north. The arrow pointing down is south. The arrow pointing left is west, and the arrow pointing right is east. We can use these directions to show the relationship, or connection, between two places.

Find Oregon and New York on this map. On the map Oregon is left of New York. This means that Oregon is west of New York. If you travel right, or east, from Oregon, you will reach New York. Have you ever heard people talking about areas of the United States, like the Northeast? The Northeast consists of states like Connecticut and Massachusetts. If you look at the map, you can see these states are in the northernmost and easternmost parts of the United States.

A political map is a representation of part of the world. Mapmakers use a scale to show how the area on the map relates to the area in the world. A scale shows the relationship between distances on a map and distances in the real world.

Most political maps use a bar scale. A bar scale shows that a certain distance on the map is equal to a different distance in the scale. The scale will tell you what that distance is. The diagram on the opposite page has a bar scale. The scale labels one of the bars as 0 miles (0 km) and the second as 300 miles (483 km). This means that the length of the space between the bars on the map equals 300 miles (483 km) in the real world.

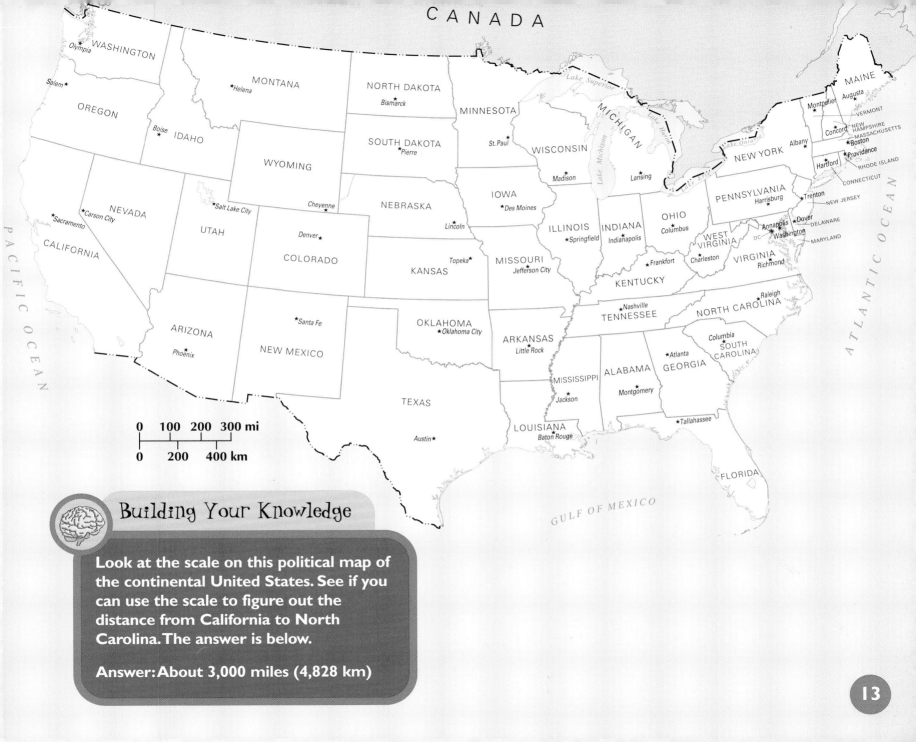

CANADA

WASHINGTON
Olympia★

Salem★
OREGON

MONTANA
★Helena

NORTH DAKOTA
Bismarck★

MINNESOTA

Lake Superior

MICHIGAN

MAINE
Augusta★
Montpelier★
VERMONT

Boise★ IDAHO

SOUTH DAKOTA
Pierre★

St.Paul★
WISCONSIN

Lake Michigan

Lake Huron

Lake Ontario

NEW HAMPSHIRE
Concord★ MASSACHUSETTS
Albany★ ★Boston
★Providence
Hartford★ RHODE ISLAND
CONNECTICUT

NEVADA
★Carson City
Sacramento★

WYOMING

★Salt Lake City

Cheyenne★

Madison★

IOWA
★Des Moines

Lansing★

Lake Erie

NEW YORK

PENNSYLVANIA
Harrisburg★

★Trenton
NEW JERSEY

CALIFORNIA

UTAH

Denver★

NEBRASKA

Lincoln★

ILLINOIS
★Springfield

INDIANA
Indianapolis★

OHIO
Columbus★

★Dover
DELAWARE

COLORADO

KANSAS

Topeka★

MISSOURI
Jefferson City★

WEST
VIRGINIA
Frankfort★ Charleston★

Annapolis★
DC★ Washington
MARYLAND

VIRGINIA
Richmond★

ARIZONA
Phoenix★

★Santa Fe

NEW MEXICO

OKLAHOMA
★Oklahoma City

ARKANSAS
Little Rock★

KENTUCKY

Nashville★
TENNESSEE

NORTH CAROLINA

Raleigh★

Columbia★
SOUTH
CAROLINA

PACIFIC OCEAN

0   100 200 300 mi

0   200   400 km

TEXAS

Austin★

MISSISSIPPI
Jackson★

ALABAMA
Montgomery★

★Atlanta
GEORGIA

ATLANTIC OCEAN

LOUISIANA
Baton Rouge★

★Tallahassee

FLORIDA

GULF OF MEXICO

Building Your Knowledge

Look at the scale on this political map of the continental United States. See if you can use the scale to figure out the distance from California to North Carolina. The answer is below.

Answer: About 3,000 miles (4,828 km)

13

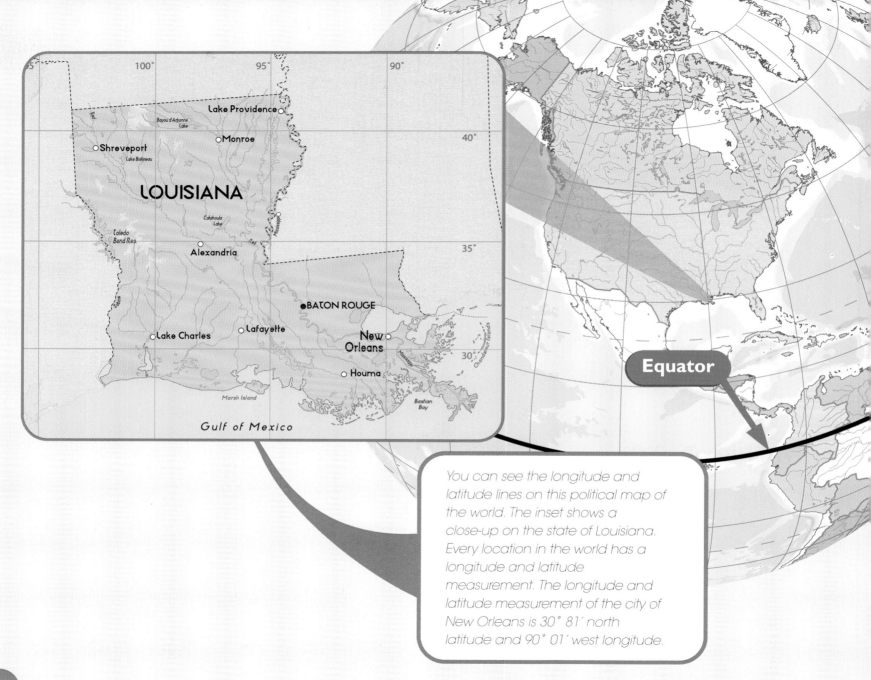

100°   95°   90°

Lake Providence

Monroe

40°

Shreveport
Lake Bistineau

LOUISIANA

Calahoula
Lake

Toledo
Bend Res.

35°

Alexandria

●BATON ROUGE

Lake Charles   Lafayette

New
Orleans

30°

Houma

Marsh Island

Bastian
Bay

Gulf of Mexico

Bayou d'Arbonne
Lake

Equator

You can see the longitude and latitude lines on this political map of the world. The inset shows a close-up on the state of Louisiana. Every location in the world has a longitude and latitude measurement. The longitude and latitude measurement of the city of New Orleans is 30° 81′ north latitude and 90° 01′ west longitude.

Latitude and Longitude

Do you know how maps show the exact location of a place on Earth? It is done by using special lines called **latitude** and **longitude**. Longitude lines run north and south. Latitude lines run east and west. The distance between latitude lines and longitude lines is measured in **degrees** and minutes. There is a longitude and latitude measurement for every location on Earth.

There are also some special longitude and latitude lines on Earth. The **prime meridian** separates the world into the Eastern **Hemisphere** and the Western Hemisphere. The prime meridian is at 0° longitude. The world is separated into the Northern Hemisphere and the Southern Hemisphere by a line at 0° latitude. This line is the **equator**. All the longitude lines meet at two points in the world. The North Pole is the northernmost point in the world. The South Pole is the southernmost.

Political maps can be used for many purposes. General political maps provide an overview of cities and political borders in an area. They can also be used to show more details or provide more facts about an area. Election maps are an example of a use of political maps. Election maps can show which states in the United States favored which **candidate** in the presidential election.

On the opposite page you can see the election map from the 2004 presidential election. The different colors represent the two candidates. George W. Bush is red and John Kerry is blue. The states that a candidate won are filled in with that color. How many states are red? How many are blue? Which candidate has a greater number of states? This political map is being used to show you the results of an election.

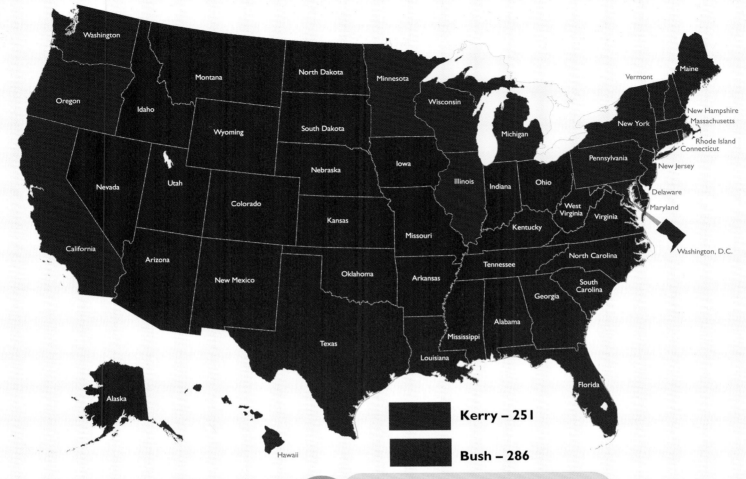

Kerry – 251

Bush – 286

 2004 Presidential Election

Building Your Knowledge

Look at this political map, which shows the results of the 2004 presidential election. The legend tells you which person the colors stand for. Each state is the color of the person who won that state. How many states did each candidate win? The answer is below.

Answer: John Kerry won 19 states and Washington, D.C. George W. Bush won 31 states.

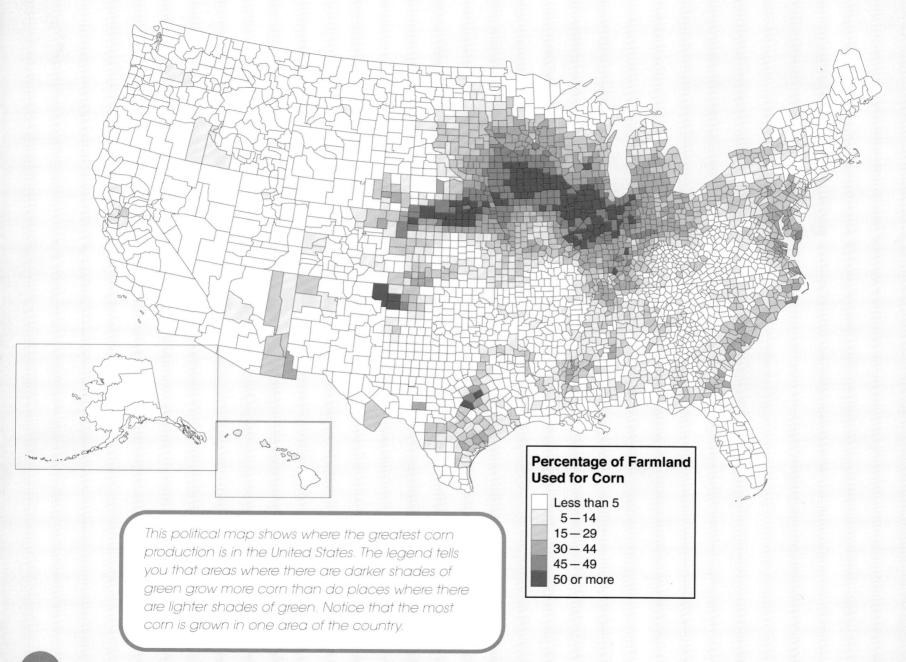

Percentage of Farmland Used for Corn

- Less than 5
- 5 — 14
- 15 — 29
- 30 — 44
- 45 — 49
- 50 or more

This political map shows where the greatest corn production is in the United States. The legend tells you that areas where there are darker shades of green grow more corn than do places where there are lighter shades of green. Notice that the most corn is grown in one area of the country.

Agricultural Maps

Agricultural maps are another type of political map. They can show us where farming areas are and what types of crops are grown there. Agricultural maps are another use of political maps. They show us how we use the land on which we live. In the United States, the Department of Agriculture reports where food is grown or produced in the United States. The department makes agricultural maps that show these facts.

On the left is an agricultural map of the United States that shows where corn is grown. The legend states that the darker shades of green are places with the highest **percentage** of their land used for corn production. From this map we can see that the most corn is grown in Illinois, Iowa, and Nebraska.

Political Maps and Road Maps

Political maps can give us a larger view of the political **landscape** of the world or an area of the world. They show cities and political borders. Political maps, however, do not show us much detail about cities. To study more detailed features of cities, other types of maps, such as road maps, are useful. Road maps show an area's roads. They also show other humanmade and natural features, such as bridges, tunnels, airports, and rivers. A political map shows that San Francisco, California, is located near the Pacific Ocean. A road map might show you where the Golden Gate Bridge is. If you look at an even more detailed road map of San Francisco, you can see the city's neighborhoods and parks and even how to drive from one area to another.

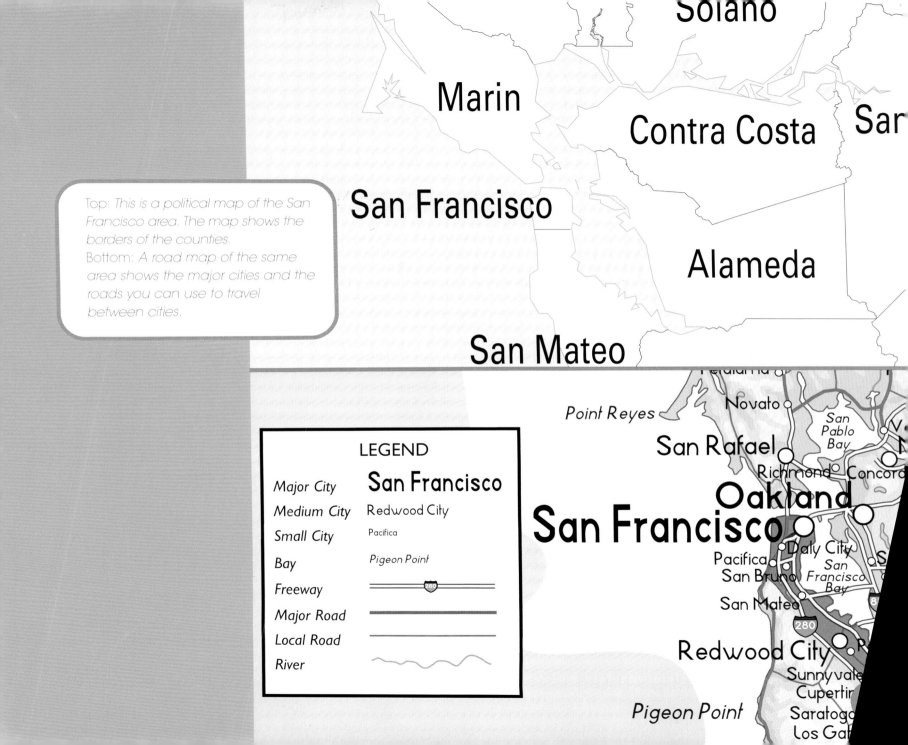

Top: *This is a political map of the San Francisco area. The map shows the borders of the counties.*
Bottom: *A road map of the same area shows the major cities and the roads you can use to travel between cities.*

Solano

Marin

Contra Costa

Sar

San Francisco

Alameda

San Mateo

LEGEND

Major City	**San Francisco**
Medium City	Redwood City
Small City	Pacifica
Bay	
	Pigeon Point
Freeway	●——280——
Major Road	——————
Local Road	——————
River	∿∿∿∿∿

Petaluma

Point Reyes

Novato

San Pablo Bay

San Rafael

Richmond Concord

Oakland

San Francisco

Pacifica
San Bruno

San Francisco Bay

Daly City

San Mateo

280

Redwood City

Pigeon Point

Sunnyvale
Cupertino
Saratoga
Los Gatos

Political maps have been used for centuries. Christopher Columbus used maps when he sailed from Spain to the Americas in 1492.

Long ago maps were drawn by hand and were not as dependable as they are today. Maps have become more exact during the past 30 years. Today political maps are drawn from pictures taken of Earth from **satellites**.

One recent advancement in mapmaking is GPS, Global Positioning System. It was created by the U.S. military to show anyone at any position on Earth exactly where he or she is. GPS uses satellites, which send directions to GPS receivers on Earth. At first only the U.S. military used them, but today GPS receivers are used throughout the world. GPS can help make more dependable political maps, which makes the maps more useful.

Glossary

agricultural maps (a-grih-KUL-chuh-rul MAPS) Maps that show farming areas.

candidate (KAN-dih-dayt) A person who runs in an election.

compass rose (KUM-pus ROHZ) A drawing on a map that shows directions.

degrees (dih-GREEZ) Measurements of longitude and latitude.

equator (ih-KWAY-tur) An imaginary line around Earth that separates it into two parts, northern and southern.

hemisphere (HEH-muh-sfeer) One half of Earth.

landscape (LAND-skayp) A view of an area.

latitude (LA-tih-tood) The distance north or south of the equator, measured by degrees.

legend (LEH-jend) A box on a map that tells what the figures on the map mean.

longitude (LON-jih-tood) The distance east or west of the prime meridian, measured by degrees.

percentage (pur-SEN-tij) Part of a whole.

physical (FIH-zih-kul) Having to do with natural forces.

political (puh-LIH-tih-kul) Having to do with the work of government or public affairs.

prime meridian (PRYM meh-RIH-dee-en) The imaginary line that passes through Greenwich, England, and that is 0° longitude.

satellites (SA-tih-lyts) Spacecraft that circle Earth.

scale (SKAYL) The measurements on a map compared to actual measurements on Earth.

symbols (SIM-bulz) Objects or pictures that stand for something else.

Index

A

agricultural maps, 19

B

bar scale, 12

C

Columbus, Christopher, 22
compass rose, 4, 11

D

directions, 4, 11

E

election maps, 16

equator, 15

G

Global Positioning System, 22

L

latitude, 15
legend, 4, 8, 19
longitude, 15

N

natural features, 7, 20
Northern Hemisphere, 15
North Pole, 15

P

political borders, 7, 16, 20
prime meridian, 15

R

relationship, 11–12
road maps, 20

S

satellites, 22
scale, 4, 12
Southern Hemisphere, 15
South Pole, 15
symbols, 4, 8

Web Sites

Due to the changing nature of Internet links, PowerKids Press has developed an online list of Web sites related to the subject of this book. This site is updated regularly. Please use this link to access the list:

www.powerkidslinks.com/mapit/political/